Did you know that less than 4,000 tigers remain in the wild? Man is the tiger's worst enemy, and every day these magnificent creatures are still being poisoned, shot and trapped to make traditional Chinese medicines and to supply the illegal wildlife trade. At the same time their natural habitat in tropical forests is being destroyed at an increasingly rapid rate. But we can also become the tiger's best friend - by refusing to buy tiger parts and products and by supporting tiger and forest conservation. Take a look at www.worldwildlife.org and www.tigersincrisis.com.

For Dads everywhere
and especially for
my father John Dermod Brennan (SB)
and my father Barry Harrison (HH)

First published in Hong Kong in 2009 by:

Auspicious
Times

Auspicious Times Limited
Room 511B, 5th Floor,
Hing Wai Centre,
7 Tin Wan Praya Road,
Tin Wan, Hong Kong
Tel: +852 9835 8074
E-mail: enquiries@auspicioustimes.com
Website: www.auspicioustimes.com

This edition published November 2010
Text copyright © Sarah Brennan 2009
Illustrations copyright © Harry Harrison 2009
Designed by e5
Produced by Macmillan Production (Asia) Ltd
Tracking Code CP-11/10
Printed in Guandong Province China
This book is printed on paper made from well-managed sustainable forest sources.

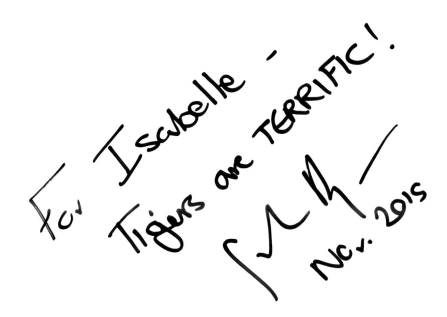

The moral right of the author and illustrator has been asserted.

ISBN: 978-988-18882-9-7

THE TALE OF
TEMUJIN

Written by
Sarah Brennan

Illustrated by
Harry Harrison

Once far away and farther on the vast Mongolian plains
Where the pastures sway like oceans in the gentle wind and rains
There was once a happy family with a mother and a dad
And a bunch of noisy children who were never cross or bad.

And they lived a life of plenty on the rich and fertile soil
With abundant game for hunting and the scantest need for toil
They were plump and plush and pretty, they had sleek and shining fur
And their favourite occupation was to lick their paws and purr.

Oh – and did I mention they were TIGERS?

Now tigers are unusual in Mongolia, 'tis true
And I doubt you'll even find one in the Ulaanbaatar zoo
For a dreadful thing once happened on that vast and fertile plain
Which discouraged any tiger from residing there again.

Some humans came a-hunting with their horses and their hounds
And their wicked bows and arrows and their sharp and shouting sounds
And they came upon the tigers in the midst of carefree play
And they shot and killed the father then they carried him away.

And in the months that followed as the mother grieved and cried
And the cubs went cold and hungry and the family nearly died
One cub alone got angry, one cub alone got mad
One cub alone vowed vengeance for the murder of his dad.

And that cub's name was Temujin.

"Temujin! Oh Temujin!" he'd hear them in his dreams
"Temujin! Oh Temujin!" he'd hear their frightened screams
"Temujin! Oh Temujin! He's coming! Lock the door!
 But most of all, block up your ears! Don't listen to his roar!"

And then he'd ROAR and all the doors would buckle to the ground
And hordes of puny human beings would scatter all around
Then one by one, he'd track them down and gobble them for tea
Together with a little dog or cat if it were free.

And so the future came to pass just as the tiger planned
For he became the fiercest beast to tread that foreign land
And when he'd munched the Mongols up he turned towards the East
And sauntered into China to continue with his feast.

And as each town was plundered and each village met its fate
He earned the name of Genghis Khan the Terrible and Great

Which is a name you may have heard before.

Now back in ancient China lay a city rich and fair
With pleasure domes and palaces bedecked with jewels rare
And beauteous parks and gardens and a very pretty lake
And every great invention that a human being can make.

The city was a masterpiece renowned from East to West
And all who lived within its walls felt well and truly blessed
Especially in the palace where the Emperor held court
The Grand Imperial Palace (or the G.I.P. for short).

The Emperor was a jolly king, his wife was good and kind
She never beat the servants and they never seemed to mind
The courtiers were gentlemen in every usual sense –
They kept their silver hidden but they gave away their pence
The fifty maids in waiting were the flowers of the realm
And everyone was happy with the Emperor at the helm

Except for her Royal Highness the Imperial Princess.

Her Royal Imperial Highness was

Precocious

Rude

Extremely

Clever

Insolent

Overbearing

Under-caring and above all

Supercilious

As princesses are wont to be especially when they're smart
With brains and beauty, too much pride and far too little heart.

So Princess Precious ruled the roost inside the G.I.P.
She played all day, she danced all night, she never ate her tea
And everything a child could want was hers at her behest
(And woe betide the palace if she didn't get the best).

Now children who are very spoilt with one too many toys
And nothing else to do but play and make a lot of noise
Are seldom happy as they seem; their life becomes a bore
Where even blowing bubblegum is just another chore.

Poor

Princess

Precious

Her life was very tough
For nothing that her parents did was ever quite enough
And every time she suffered she would make them suffer too
(Which, when your name is Precious, is the only thing to do.)

One fateful summer morning in that city rich and fair
The citizens awoke to worried whispers in the air
They heard them at the city walls, they heard them at the Gate
And rumours rippled round the town of Genghis Khan the Great.

"Temujin! Oh Temujin!" the people cried in fear
"Temujin! Oh Temujin! They say he's very near!"
"Temujin! Oh Temujin! He's coming! Lock the door!
But most of all, block up your ears! Don't listen to his roar!"

But then he ROARED and all the walls came tumbling down inside
While all the townsfolk ran away to find a place to hide
But one by one he found them, ate them up, then took a rest
(Ten thousand human beings take some hours to digest).

Meanwhile, back in the G.I.P., the young princess was glum
She'd rung the bell for morning tea but nobody had come
She stamped her foot and rang again but no one seemed to heed
It was the *very* treatment that a princess didn't need.

She threw a little tantrum but it fizzled in mid-air
(A tantrum is a rather silly thing when no one's there)
The palace was as silent as a mighty Emperor's tomb
And no one saw the Princess as she tiptoed from the room.

She tiptoed past the bedrooms then she slithered down the stairs
She shimmied past the study with its rampant panda bears
She crept along the corridor then slid along the wall
Until at last she made it to the Grand Imperial Hall.

And there, in golden splendour, stood the Grand Imperial Gong
Which no one EVER used except when Things Went Awfully Wrong

Which, in the Princess's humble opinion, they had.

"BONG!!!" the Princess whacked it with her Most Imperial Might
It echoed through the palace to the left and to the right
Then up into the rafters and down through every drain
And on and on it echoed as the Princess bonged again.

Now Temujin was sleeping by the famous G.I.P.
As Princess Precious fretted for her missing morning tea
But when the gong resounded in his hot and heavy head
He thought it might be sensible to get up out of bed.

He stretched and yawned and grumbled as the gong rang out again
That ringing sound was starting to become a royal pain
And so he quietly padded through the broken palace wall
And followed the commotion to the Grand Imperial Hall

Which, as we all know, is where the Princess was banging away in a very bad mood.

The Princess was not happy; she was far from being amused
She wasn't used to having things like morning tea refused
But then the door swung open and a shadow drifted in
The Princess turned to yell at it...and there stood Temujin.

'I want my tea!" snapped Precious with a Most Imperial Glare
The tiger turned to fix her with his most ferocious stare
"I want it, and I want it NOW!" she gave a haughty flounce
The tiger licked his lips and crouched in readiness to pounce.

'Are you STILL here?" the princess cried "You're FIRED! Go pack your bags!"
But Temujin just leered at her and gave his tail a wag.

And then...and then...I scarcely dare repeat what happened next
I guess it's only natural when a creature's being vexed
But it was truly horrible, disgusting and insane...
The tiger leapt into the air...and Precious yelled again.

Only this time she really, really lost it.

screamed Princess Precious as the tiger left the ground
It was the most *appalling* sort of *screeching* sort of sound
Poor Temujin was thunderstruck! It froze him in mid-air
Then swiftly threw him backwards till he landed in a chair!

AGH!

His eyes were glazed with terror and his jaws were wide and slack
His every hair was standing on his arched and rigid back
But as his senses rallied and his wits returned once more

The tiger turned on Precious with his most SPECTACULAR roar

And this is how it went:

Miaooooooooow!

Miaow!

Poor Temujin was horrified! He'd lost his famous roar!
He'd lost the very thing that he was most respected for!
He looked at Princess Precious, Princess Precious looked at him
They both looked at each other…then they both began to grin!

And then they started giggling till the tears ran down like rain
And Precious called out *"Kitty!"* and the tiger miaowed again.

So what became of Temujin, that most ferocious beast
To Genghis Khan the Terrible, the terror of the East?
And what became of Precious till the end of all *her* days
With her boredom and her tantrums and her silly royal ways?

Well, here's a little secret: - There's a song they're singing still
From the Himalayan mountains to the Baba-Wali hills
And the dusty Gobi Desert where it hardly ever rains
And the Yangtze River delta and the vast Mongolian plains

"Temujin! Oh Temujin!" you'll hear the old folks sing
"Temujin! Oh Temujin! Oh Mighty Tiger King!
Temujin! Oh Temujin! Put out a bowl of cream!
But most of all, block up your ears! Don't listen to that SCREAM!"

Sarah Brennan

Sarah Brennan is the author of the popular Dirty Story series and of the best-selling Chinese Calendar Tales, all illustrated by Harry Harrison. Born in Tasmania, Australia, she grew up on the slopes of Mount Wellington surrounded by bush animals, goats and exotic poultry. She also played the bagpipes (at the very bottom of the garden) and wrote lots of stories and poems which she kept in a big pink plastic bag! Sarah worked for ten years as a medical lawyer in London before moving to Hong Kong in 1998. She is also the author of the seditiously naughty parenting advice manual *Dummies for Mummies: What to Expect When You're Least Expecting.* Sarah lives in Hong Kong with her French husband, two daughters and an opinionated cocker spaniel, visiting China, Singapore, the UK and Australia on a regular basis.

Visit Sarah Brennan's funny and fabulous website at www.sarah-brennan.com.
You can follow Sarah's blog on http://sarahbrennanblog.wordpress.com.

Harry Harrison

Robert Harrison, nicknamed "Harry", grew up with a Dad in the air force, so he lived in lots of different places including Singapore and Libya before settling down in West London. As a boy, Harry loved insects, exploring, climbing trees, making dens and playing war, but he didn't like sport! He has been drawing for as long as he can remember, but he's never had any formal art training.

Harry worked as a freelance illustrator in Sydney and London before settling in Hong Kong, where he became the iconic *Harry*, political cartoonist for the *South China Morning Post*. He is also a regular contributor to The Guardian, the Wall Street Journal, Time magazine, the International Finance Review and the Far Eastern Economic Review. He lives with his wife, son, daughter and restlessly senile cat on Lamma Island in Hong Kong.

See more of Harry Harrison's wild and wacky illustrations on http://www.flickr.com/photos/harryharrisonillos.

Genghis Khan

Genghis Khan was perhaps the greatest warrior the world has ever seen. Born in Mongolia in around 1165, he was the third son of a minor tribal chief and was named Temujin, pronounced *Tem-o-jin*, after a Tatar warrior his father had just captured. When Temujin was 9, his father was killed by a rival clan and the family was abandoned by their tribe. But Temujin was clever and resourceful, gaining a reputation for bravery and making strategic alliances as he grew older. Gradually he built up a force of loyal followers who helped him to unite the Mongol tribes and by 1206 he was crowned Genghis Khan, or Universal King. His army went on to invade China and Central Asia, so that by the time of his death in 1227, he had created an empire which spread from the Sea of Japan in the East to the Caspian Sea in the West! Love him or hate him, his name will never be forgotten.